FUN FACT FILE:
INVENTIONS THAT CHANGED THE WORLD

20 FUN FACTS ABOUT THE PRINTING PRESS

BY DANIELLE HAYNES

Gareth Stevens PUBLISHING

Please visit our website, www.garethstevens.com. For a free color catalog of all our high-quality books, call toll free 1-800-542-2595 or fax 1-877-542-2596.

Library of Congress Cataloging-in-Publication Data
Names: Haynes, Danielle, author.
Title: 20 fun facts about the printing press / Danielle Haynes.
Other titles: Twenty fun facts about the printing press
Description: Buffalo, New York : Gareth Stevens Publishing, [2024] | Series: Fun fact file. Inventions that changed the world | Includes bibliographical references and index.
Identifiers: LCCN 2022060230 (print) | LCCN 2022060231 (ebook) | ISBN 9781538287712 (library binding) | ISBN 9781538287705 (paperback) | ISBN 9781538287729 (ebook)
Subjects: LCSH: Printing presses–History–Juvenile literature. | Printing–History–Juvenile literature.
Classification: LCC Z124 .H39 2024 (print) | LCC Z124 (ebook) | DDC 686.209–dc23/eng/20230104
LC record available at https://lccn.loc.gov/2022060230
LC ebook record available at https://lccn.loc.gov/2022060231

Published in 2024 by
Gareth Stevens Publishing
2544 Clinton Street
Buffalo, NY 14224

Designer: Leslie Taylor
Editor: Therese Shea

Photo credits: Cover, p. 1 (main) silvano audisio/Shutterstock.com; Series Art (file folder) David Smart/Shutterstock.com, (binder clip) luckyraccoon/Shutterstock.com, (wood grain background) ARENA Creative/Shutterstock.com; p. 5 Tania Zbrodko/Shutterstock.com; p. 6 Naturehead/https://commons.wikimedia.org/wiki/File:Dharani_sutra.jpg; p. 7 Anna Kepa/Shutterstock.com; p. 8 Classic Image/Alamy.com; p. 9 Everett Collection/Shutterstock.com; p. 10 (scribe) Jean Le Tavernier/https://commons.wikimedia.org/wiki/File:The_Scribe_at_Work.jpg, (manuscript) Virag Nobile/Shutterstock.com; p. 11 Osugi/Shutterstock.com; p. 12 DaLiu/Shutterstock.com; p. 13 J J Osuna Caballero/Shutterstock.com; p. 14 Fallaner/https://commons.wikimedia.org/wiki/File:Diocesan_Museum_in_Pelplin_2019_P01.jpg; p. 15 https://commons.wikimedia.org/wiki/File:Studying_astronomy_and_geometry.jpg; p. 16 Stig Alenas/Shutterstock.com; p. 17 Torben Knauer/Shutterstock.com; p. 18 https://commons.wikimedia.org/wiki/File:Relation_Aller_Fuernemmen_und_gedenckwuerdigen_Historien_(1609).jpg; p. 19 Derek Skinner/Shutterstock.com; p. 20 Daderot/https://commons.wikimedia.org/wiki/File:Kittredge_Hall_-_Harvard_University_-_DSC01440.jpg; p. 21 User:Parhamr/https://commons.wikimedia.org/wiki/File:Koenig%27s_steam_press_-_1814.png; p. 22 Historical Images Archive/Alamy.com; p. 23 zefart/Shutterstock.com; p. 24 (portrait) Mathew Benjamin Brady/https://commons.wikimedia.org/wiki/File:Richard_March_Hoe_-_Brady-Handy.jpg, (press) Bolles, Albert Sidney/https://commons.wikimedia.org/wiki/File:Web-perfecting_newspaper_printing_machine.jpg; p. 26 sirtravelalot/Shutterstock.com; p. 27 Antonio Guillem/Shutterstock.com; p. 29 wavebreakmedia/Shutterstock.com.

Printed in the United States of America

CPSIA compliance information: Batch #CSGS24: For further information contact Gareth Stevens at 1-800-542-2595.

CONTENTS

Words in the glossary appear in **bold** type the first time they are used in the text.

CHANGING LIVES

Today, books, newspapers, and magazines are everywhere you look, and most people can read them. But before the printing press, few people could read. Many think this makes the printing press one of the most important inventions of all time!

Long ago, books were handwritten, which made them costly. The printing press made it quicker and cheaper to produce books and other **texts**. That meant more people could own books. And more and more people learned to read. This led them to learn more, share ideas more, and even question their leaders.

The first printing presses were completely manual. That means they were operated by people rather than by electricity or other power.

BEGINNINGS IN ASIA

FUN FACT: 1

NO ONE KNOWS WHEN THE PRINTING PRESS WAS INVENTED.

Many think German Johannes Gutenberg invented the first one. But people in today's China were using **woodblocks** to print for hundreds of years before him. And Koreans used metal **type** before Gutenberg did too.

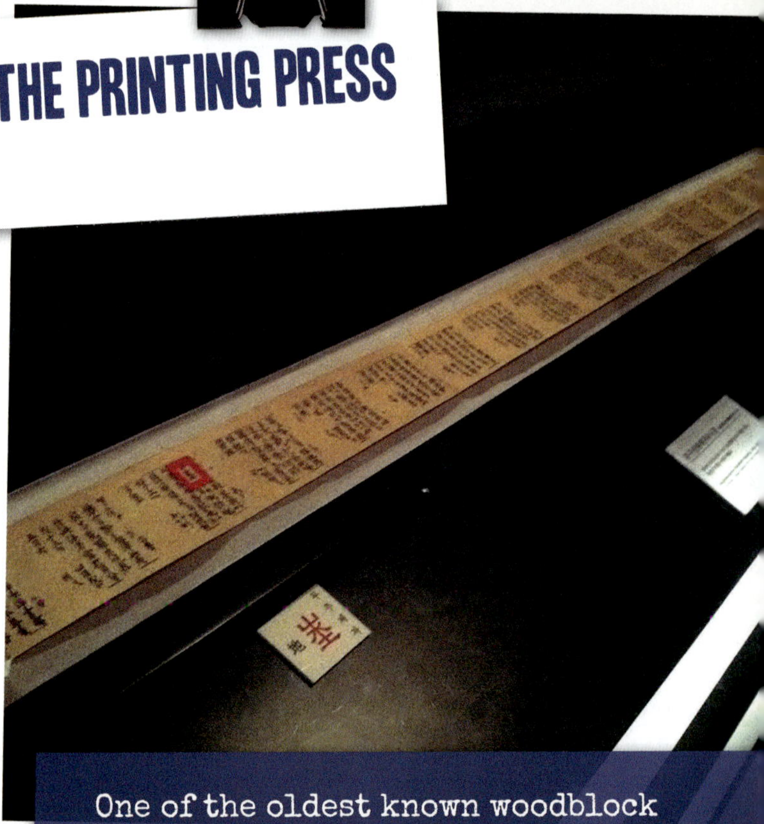

One of the oldest known woodblock prints in the world is a text called the *Pure Light Dharani-sutra*. Scientists believe it was printed in the eighth century in what is now South Korea.

Even though carving woodblocks takes time and effort, it's still used to create art and other printed items.

FUN FACT: 2

IN THE OLDEST FORM OF PRINTING, EACH PAGE WAS CARVED ENTIRELY BY HAND.

This printing used woodblocks. To make a print, someone would carve text on wood. They'd put ink on the wood and lay paper over it. The text **transferred** to the paper.

The Chinese language has tens of thousands of characters compared to 26 letters in English. That's a lot of individual pieces of type to carve!

FUN FACT: 3

THE CREATOR OF THE FIRST MOVEABLE-TYPE PRINTING PRESS LIVED ABOUT 1,000 YEARS AGO IN CHINA.

Chinese **alchemist** Pi Sheng used clay and glue to make individual characters. The characters could be put together to make a page of text.

JOHANNES GUTENBERG

FUN FACT: 4

JOHANNES GUTENBERG DIDN'T INVENT THE PRINTING PRESS, BUT HE REVOLUTIONIZED IT!

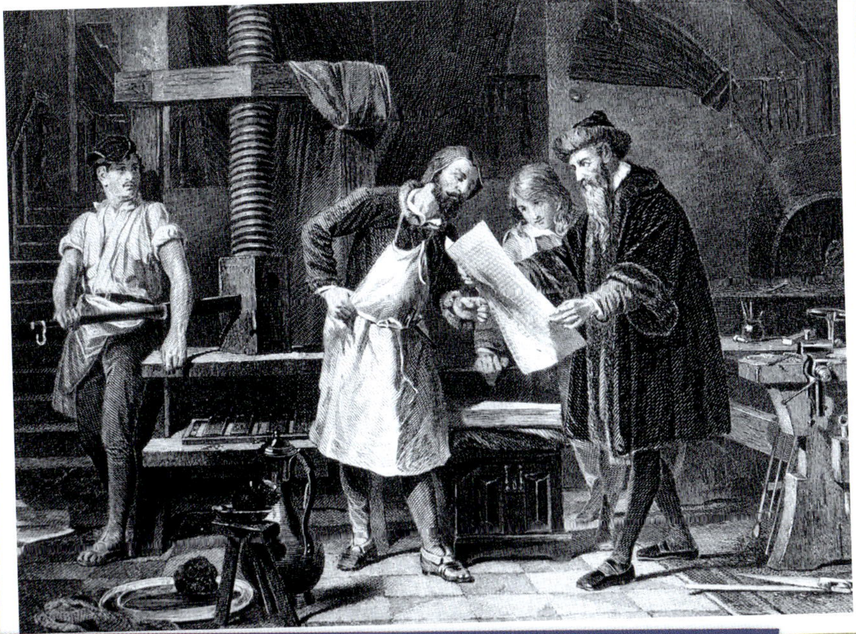

Before inventing the printing press, Gutenberg was a metalworker. Metal type lasts longer than wooden or clay type.

By 1450, Gutenberg combined existing ideas with some new ones of his own to create a new kind of printing press. It used a special metal type instead of clay or wood type.

FUN FACT: 5

BEFORE GUTENBERG'S PRESS, SCRIBES COULD SPEND A WHOLE YEAR COPYING A SINGLE BOOK BY HAND!

Scribes were usually monks, or religious men who live apart from society. They copied two to three pages by hand each day. These books were called illuminated manuscripts.

Illuminated manuscripts were often decorated with fancy letters and drawings in the **margins.**

Each page of the Gutenberg Bible had two **columns** of 42 lines of text. It's also known as the *Forty-Two Line Bible*.

FUN FACT: 6

EACH GUTENBERG BIBLE WEIGHS ABOUT 14 POUNDS (6.4 KG)!

The Bible was the first book Gutenberg printed using his press. He printed only 180 copies, each of which used 300 different pieces of type. Forty-nine incomplete or full copies exist today.

FUN FACT: 7

IN THE 50 YEARS AFTER GUTENBERG'S INVENTION, THE NUMBER OF BOOKS IN EUROPE GREW FROM ABOUT 30,000 TO MORE THAN 9 MILLION.

With the invention of the printing press, books became more **accessible** to all people, not just the rich.

The printing press allowed books to be printed much faster and cheaper than when they were copied by hand.

THE GUTENBERG PRINTING PRESS

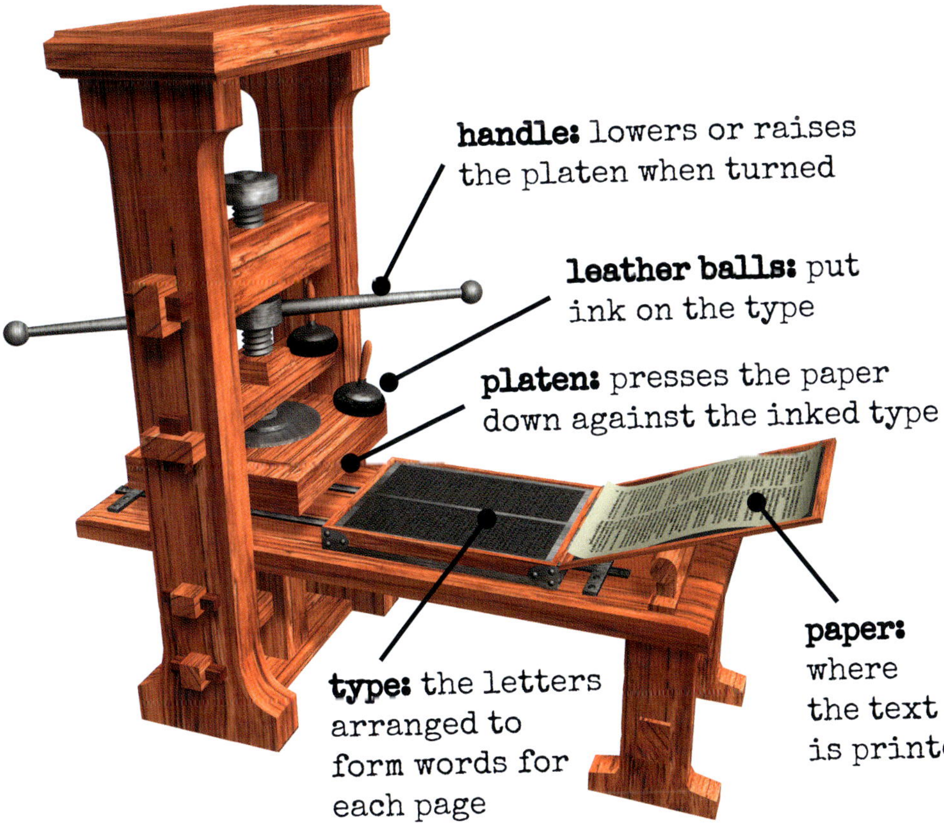

Gutenberg's press used metal type that could melt and cool quickly.

FUN FACT: 8

A SINGLE VOLUME OF THE GUTENBERG BIBLE SOLD FOR $5.39 MILLION IN 1987!

The Gutenberg Bible was so big, it was split into two volumes.

Experts think if a complete Bible came up for sale today, it could sell for $35 million. That's enough money to buy 70,000 PlayStation 5s, 8 million comic books, or 55 million pounds (25 million kg) of bananas.

READING REVOLUTION

FUN FACT: 9

BEFORE THE PRINTING PRESS, MOST EUROPEANS WERE ILLITERATE, MEANING THEY COULDN'T READ.

Because most people couldn't read, the Catholic Church had power over what people knew and believed through its teachings.

Only the wealthy, upper classes usually had the time to learn to read or the money to afford books. Most Europeans only learned about the world and religion through traveling merchants or the Catholic Church.

FUN FACT: 10

THE PRINTING PRESS CHANGED RELIGION IN EUROPE FOREVER!

More people learned to read and had access to cheaper books. German priest Martin Luther was able to reach more people with ideas about reforming, or changing, the Catholic Church.

Martin Luther was **excommunicated** from the Catholic Church in 1521 for his writings against the Church.

Legend has it that Luther nailed his *Ninety-Five Theses* to the door of All Saints' Church in Wittenberg in what is now Germany in 1517.

FUN FACT: 11

HISTORIANS CONSIDER MARTIN LUTHER TO BE THE WORLD'S FIRST BEST-SELLING AUTHOR.

The German priest's **pamphlet**, *Ninety-Five Theses*, called for reforms of the Catholic Church. Luther's other writings and books became popular and changed Christianity forever. He also wrote an edition of the New Testament in German.

SPREADING THE NEWS

FUN FACT: 12

THE OLDEST SURVIVING COPY OF A PRINTED NEWSPAPER IS MORE THAN 400 YEARS OLD!

German printer Johann Carolus created the first weekly newspaper in 1605. It had a very long name in German—*Relation Aller Fürnemmen und Gedenckwürdigen Historien*—but some historians just call it the *Relation*.

R 105 652

Relation:

Aller Fürnem-
men/vnd gedenckwürdigen
Historien / so sich hin vnnd wider
in Hoch vnnd Nieder Teutschland / auch
in Franckreich / Italien / Schott vnd Engelland /
Hispanien / Hungern / Polen / Siebenbürgen /
Wallachey / Moldaw / Türckey / etc. Inn
diesem 1609. Jahr verlauffen
vnd zutragen möchte.

Alles auff das trewlichst wie
ich solche bekommen vnd zu wegen
bringen mag / in Truck ver-
fertigen will.

The *Relation*'s full title means *Account of All Distinguished and Commemorable News*. The oldest copy dates to 1609. It's kept at the University of Heidelberg in Germany.

Printers had to be really good at spelling and arranging words backward—and sometimes upside down!

FUN FACT: 13

PRINTERS PUT NEWSPAPERS AND BOOKS TOGETHER IN REVERSE!

Each character or letter must be made in reverse for both woodblock and moveable-type printing. Words must also be spelled backward. Paper placed on the carved type or block picks up the image in the way it would be read.

PRINTING MILESTONES

FUN FACT: 14

IN 1638, ELIZABETH GLOVER BROUGHT THE FIRST PRINTING PRESS TO BRITAIN'S COLONIES IN AMERICA.

It was the second press in North America, the first having arrived in Mexico in 1539. When Glover died in 1643, she left her press to Harvard University.

Harvard University Press was founded in 1913, but Glover's original press has since been lost to time.

Koenig's press used cylinders, or drums, that rolled the paper onto inked type, instead of using a flat platen. This was called a rotary printing press.

FUN FACT: 15

GERMAN INVENTOR FRIEDRICH KOENIG USED STEAM TO POWER A PRINTING PRESS IN 1811.

Instead of requiring humans to operate the press, Koenig's invention used steam to make the machine move. The new press could print 1,000 pages per hour.

IN FULL COLOR

FUN FACT: 16

IN 1842, THE *ILLUSTRATED LONDON NEWS* BECAME THE FIRST NEWSPAPER TO REGULARLY INCLUDE IMAGES, OR PICTURES, NOT JUST WORDS.

The *Illustrated London News* was a weekly newspaper. Presses had printed drawings before this, but no other newspapers printed as many images, like newspapers do today.

The *Illustrated London News* also became the first newspaper to publish, or print, color images, with its special Christmas paper in 1855.

In color printing, the paper receives a layer each of cyan (a greenish-blue), magenta (a pinkish-purple), yellow, and black to create a full image.

FUN FACT: 17

COLOR PRINTING USES THREE BRIGHT COLORS—CYAN, MAGENTA, AND YELLOW—AND BLACK.

Printing presses use a combination of these colors at different **transparencies** to create any other color needed. The method is based on ideas about color by painter Jakob Christof Le Blon in the 18th century.

MILES AND MILES OF PAPER

FUN FACT: 18

AMERICAN RICHARD M. HOE INVENTED A WAY FOR PRINTING PRESSES TO USE A PAPER ROLL 5 MILES (8 KM) LONG INSTEAD OF SEPARATE SHEETS.

His invention, first used in 1870, was called a Hoe web perfecting press. It allowed the *New York Tribune* newspaper to print 18,000 papers per hour!

The rotary printing press works by passing the long sheet of paper along a cylinder with a printing plate. Other drums called impression cylinders press the paper against the printing plate.

THE ROTARY PRINTING PRESS

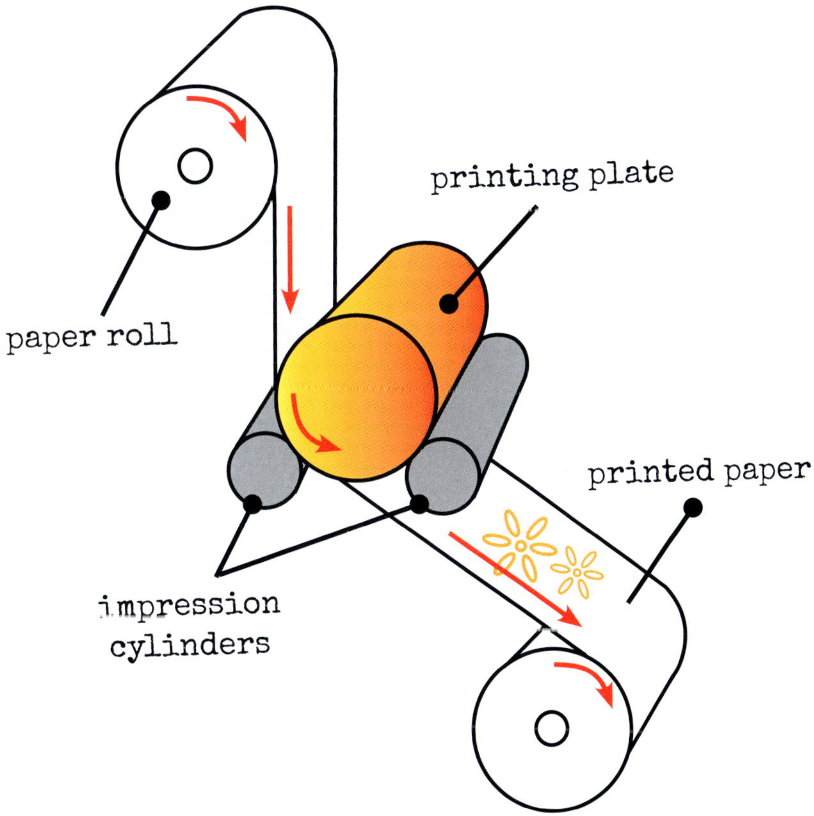

Later rotary presses could cut and fold the paper after it was printed.

HIGH-TECH PRINTING

FUN FACT: 19

TODAY, PRINTING PRESSES PRODUCE MORE THAN 24 MILLION INDIVIDUAL NEWSPAPERS EACH DAY IN THE UNITED STATES!

That may seem like a lot, but print numbers have gone down. They hit a height of about 63 million in 1984. More and more people get the news online or from TV.

Current newspaper printing presses are much bigger than the Gutenberg press. One of the largest today is called the Mitsubishi DIAMONDSTAR, which is four stories tall!

Some modern printers don't even use a press. You might even have a small printer in your own home.

FUN FACT: 20

MODERN PRINTING PRESSES USE COMPUTERS TO DO A LOT OF THE WORK.

Presses no longer have people to arrange the type for each page or carve plates for drawings. All this work is done on computers. The printing plates are now made with lasers!

LASTING LEGACY

It's hard to believe the small printers in our homes and giant newspaper presses that fill entire buildings share a common history. Even more unbelievable is the fact that it all started with simple hand-carved woodblocks.

Millions of people have printers in their homes to print photos or homework. And yet, not that long ago in human history, most people couldn't read. Imagine all the other inventions we wouldn't have if the printing press hadn't spread knowledge!

Today, libraries are full of millions of books, magazines, newspapers, and other printed material.

GLOSSARY

accessible: Easy to get.

alchemist: A person who uses or studies a seemingly magical form of science.

carve: To form an object by cutting and shaping a material such as wood.

column: A section of print that appears next to another on a page and is separated from it by a line or space.

excommunicate: To kick out from a church or other group.

margin: The space around the outside of a printed page.

pamphlet: A small book that gives information.

reverse: To change the position of something.

revolutionize: Causing a great or complete change.

text: The main body of words in a book, newspaper, or other printed matter.

transfer: To move something from one place to another.

transparency: Being transparent, or letting light shine through.

type: A piece of metal or wood that has a letter or character carved into it.

woodblock: A block of wood that has an image or text carved into it.

FOR MORE INFORMATION

BOOKS

Dufresne, Emilie. *News and the Media.* New York, NY: Enslow Publishing, 2021.

Miller, Derek. *A Day With a Librarian.* New York, NY: Cavendish Square, 2020.

Miller, Derek. *Books.* New York, NY: Cavendish Square, 2020.

WEBSITES

Biography: Johannes Gutenberg
www.ducksters.com/biography/johannes_gutenberg.php
Read about inventor Johannes Gutenberg and the famous Bible he printed.

Newspaper Facts for Kids
kids.kiddle.co/Newspaper
Learn about the sections of a newspaper, and look at photos of famous newspapers through history.

Printing Press
kids.britannica.com/kids/article/printing-press/627243
Learn how the printing press works and its impact on how people share information.

Publisher's note to educators and parents: Our editors have carefully reviewed these websites to ensure that they are suitable for students. Many websites change frequently, however, and we cannot guarantee that a site's future contents will continue to meet our high standards of quality and educational value. Be advised that students should be closely supervised whenever they access the internet.

INDEX